JEREMY THE BIBLE BOOKWORM
TELLS ABOUT THE
LIFE of JESUS

Written by **Roberta Letwenko**
Illustrated by **Edward Letwenko**

Regina Press New York

Jeremy and his friends had been busy all morning building their playhouse. "I can't wait until it's finished," said Jennie Bee. "It'll be such fun having our own special house to play in." "It can be our secret meeting place," added Basil.

The three Ladybug children carried small bundles of dried grass to cover the floor of the tiny house. "I think that's a little heavy for you," said Jennie to Baby Ladybug as she lifted the bundle from Baby's arms. "Let me help."

"I can do it," said Baby. But no one heard.

"We've got to decide what to use for a roof," said Jeremy. "Any ideas?" The field children excitedly shared ideas about their playhouse.

"I think big shiny leaves would be perfect," said Baby Ladybug. But no one heard.

"Let's have a party when our house is finished," said Basil. "Jennie, maybe you can bring some honey."

"I will," said Jennie, "and we can have some fresh berries."

"We'll bring those," Jimmy and Johnny Ladybug shouted together.

"I just love berries," said Baby Ladybug. But no one heard.

As the others discussed their plans, Baby Ladybug walked away sadly — and no one noticed.

Later that day, the small group of field children stood proudly in front of their creation.

"It's beautiful," said Jennie.

"A perfect job, if I do say so myself," said Jeremy. And everyone agreed.

"Let's try it out," said Jimmy, and the children all went into the house.

"It's a perfect fit for the six of us," said Johnny.

"You're right," agreed Basil, looking around, "but there are only five of us."

Jeremy counted out loud, "One, two, three, four, five, someone is missing."

"It's Baby," said Jennie. "Where's Baby?"

The field children rushed out of the playhouse, calling and looking for Baby. Baby Ladybug was nowhere in sight.

"Baby has never gone far from home," Johnny and Jimmy said together. "We're worried!"

"Let's organize a search," said Jennie. "We'll each go in a different direction. That way we'll find Baby for sure."

They all scurried off in search of the tiny ladybug.

Jeremy walked a long time through the prairie grass. "Baby! Baby!" he called as he walked.

"He couldn't have come this far," Jeremy thought out loud. "I guess I'd better turn back."

Just then he heard a small voice, crying. "Jeremy, is that you?" the voice said softly.

Jeremy ran to the sound, and there, on a small stone, sat
Baby Ladybug. His eyes were filled with tears.

"Oh, Jeremy. I was so scared!"

"What happened?" Jeremy asked. "We've looked everywhere
for you."

"Well," began Baby, "everyone was busy with the playhouse. I wanted to help, but no one would let me. I'm not as strong as the others, and because I'm small nobody listens to me. I felt sad because I'm too small to help. So I just started walking and thinking, and then — I got lost!" He began to cry again.

Jeremy gave Baby a hug.

"Don't you know you're special just the way you are? God made you exactly the way you ought to be. And God has a special plan for you too."

"For me?" asked Baby. "But I'm so small."

"Of course," Jeremy answered. "Why, God's very own Son Jesus came to us as a tiny baby, and God already had a special plan for him. Would you like to hear about it, Baby?"

"Oh yes, Jeremy," he answered, "but please don't call me Baby anymore. My name is Joey."

Jeremy smiled. "Well Joey...

"Baby Jesus was born in a cave in the city of Bethlehem. His parents, Mary and Joseph, knew that Jesus was special right from the start.

"Shepherds outside of town heard about Jesus from angels singing in the night. As soon as those shepherds heard the news, they came to see the new baby. And in far off countries, a special bright star led a group of Wise Men to Bethlehem. They came with wonderful gifts for Jesus.

"Jesus grew up in a village called Nazareth. Joseph was a carpenter, and Jesus learned how to work with wood. Each day Mary and Joseph read the Bible to Jesus. Jesus loved hearing those stories about God."

"I like to hear about God, too!" said Joey.

Jeremy continued, "When Jesus was twelve, Mary and Joseph took him to the city of Jerusalem for a big celebration called Passover. On the way back, they looked for Jesus and couldn't find him. They thought he was lost."

"I'll bet they were worried," said Joey.

"They were," Jeremy answered, "just like we all were worried about you, Joey. But Mary and Joseph went back to Jerusalem and found Jesus in the holy Temple. He was talking to the teachers about the Bible. Those teachers were surprised at how much Jesus knew about God.

"Jesus always knew that God had a plan for his life. When he grew up, he left his home in Nazareth to travel around telling the people about God's wonderful love.

"But first he went down to the Jordan River where a man called John the Baptist was blessing people in the river. John told the people to get ready for someone special, someone who was coming to save God's people.

"When Jesus stepped into the river, John was surprised. Why would God's own Son come to be baptized? And when John poured water over Jesus' head, a dove flew down and God's voice said 'This is my Son. I love him very much.'"

Joey smiled. "I'll bet it made Jesus happy to hear that."

"We all like to know we're loved," said Jeremy.

He went on. "As Jesus traveled, he called others to join him. He chose twelve men to be his special helpers. They were called the apostles.

"Jesus asked the apostles to leave their homes and families and follow him, to help him spread the good news about God's love."

"That would be hard to do," said Joey.

"Yes, but they were happy with Jesus," said Jeremy.

"Jesus especially loved little children. Wherever he went, he always welcomed the little ones and gave them his special blessing."

"I'm glad Jesus thinks children are special." Joey said smiling.

"Whenever Jesus spoke about God, crowds gathered around to hear him. He would sit on a lake shore or on a hillside or in someone's house and talk about God for hours.

"One day thousands of people were listening to Jesus for a long time. Jesus knew the people were hungry and wanted to feed them.

"One little boy had five loaves of bread and two fish, and he gave them to Jesus. Jesus blessed the loaves and fish and told the apostles to share them with the people. The loaves and fish kept multiplying until all those people had had their fill. And there were twelve baskets of food left over. Can you imagine that, Joey?"

"Wow!" said Joey. "Only God's Son could do something like that."

"That's right," Jeremy answered.

"Another time, when Jesus and his friends were crossing the lake in a boat, a terrible storm came up. Jesus was asleep in the boat. The apostles were afraid they would all drown so they woke Jesus.

"Jesus stood up, stretched out his arms, and spoke to the wind and the sea. The storm stopped as soon as he spoke. He wanted his friends to trust him."

"If I was in that boat with Jesus, I wouldn't be afraid," Joey said bravely.

"Jesus said we should love our neighbors as much as we love ourselves. He once told the story about a traveler who was robbed and beaten along the road. People came along that road and passed him right by. Only one man stopped to help him. They call that man the Good Samaritan because he was from a town called Samaria. The Good Samaritan cared for the man and took him to a safe place.

"Sometimes Jesus showed God's love by healing people who were sick or hurting in some way. He could make the lame get up and walk and the blind look out and see. Wherever Jesus went, crowds gathered around him.

"Once, some men brought a very sick friend to the house where Jesus was speaking. They wanted Jesus to cure him. The man could not even stand. He could only lie on his mat and pray to get better.

"The man's friends couldn't get past the crowds and into the house. So they made a hole in the roof above Jesus and lowered the sick man down. Jesus was pleased to see that they had such great faith in God. He said to the sick man, 'Pick up your bed and walk.' And the man was cured — just like that!"

"Jesus must love people very much," said Joey.

"Sometimes Jesus even brought people who had died back to life. Once a man begged Jesus to cure his sick little girl. Jesus went with the man, but by the time they got to the house, the little girl had died. Her parents were in tears.

" 'Don't cry,' Jesus said. 'She isn't dead, she is only sleeping.' Jesus took the little girl by the hand and told her to get up. Then he told her parents to give her something to eat.

"Jesus talked a lot about God's forgiveness. He once told a story about a man with two sons. One son stayed with his father and helped him. The other son left home and went far away. After a while, he knew that he'd made a mistake. He was out of money and out of friends. He was hungry and lonely. So he decided to go home. His father saw him coming and ran down the road to welcome him back. Jesus said that story is about God. Like a loving Father, God forgives us when we make mistakes.

"God loves everyone, Joey, down to the smallest creature. He has a special place and a special plan for each of us — and he sent his Son Jesus to show us the way to live and love in our world."

Jeremy looked up. The sky was turning pink with the setting sun.

"Goodness, Joey," he said, "it's getting late. We'd better start for home."

"Okay," said Joey. "Jeremy, I hope the others don't laugh at me because I got lost."

"Oh, we don't have to tell them you got lost, Joey," Jeremy said with a smile. "We'll say you went looking for things for our playhouse."

Joey jumped down off the rock. "But that's true," he said, "and I found something, too. Look over here."

He led Jeremy to a patch of tall field grass. He pushed the grass apart, and there was an old flower pot with a crack in the side, just the right size for small creatures to crawl into.

"If we use this for our playhouse, we can play inside all year, even on cold and rainy days," said Joey.

"It's great!" said Jeremy. "It's even better than the one we made. We'll come back tomorrow with the others and take it home. Now we'd better get going."

The two friends reached the field just as it was getting dark. Mrs. Ladybug stood talking with the other children. When they saw Joey and Jeremy, they ran over to greet them.

"We were so worried!" said Jennie.

"Where were you, Baby?" Jimmy and Johnny asked together.

"JOEY," Jeremy said loudly, giving the others a special look, "found something for our playhouse. Tell them, Joey."

"Yes, Joey, what did you find?" asked Mrs. Ladybug. Joey told them about his exciting discovery — and everyone listened.

That night Mrs. Ladybug tucked her children into bed. "Good night, Jimmy," she said, and gave Jimmy a hug.

"Good night, Johnny," she said, and gave Johnny a hug.

"And good night, Joey," she said, and gave Joey a hug — then she whispered in Joey's ear, "but in my heart, you will always be my baby."

Joey smiled — and felt very special.